THE SECRETS TO
RULING SCHOOL

THE SECRETS TO

RU[...]
SCH[...]

AMULET BOOKS
NEW YORK

ING OOL

WITHOUT EVEN TRYING

NEIL SWAAB

Library of Congress Cataloging-in-Publication Data

Swaab, Neil, author, illustrator.

The secrets to ruling school (without even trying) / by Neil Swaab.

pages cm. — ([Max Corrigan ; 1])

ISBN 978-1-4197-1221-0 (hardback) — ISBN 978-1-61312-836-7 (ebook)

[1. Middle schools—Fiction. 2. Schools—Fiction.

3. Interpersonal relations—Fiction.

4. Humorous stories.] I. Title.

PZ7.1.S92Rul 2015

[Fic]—dc23

2015002499

Text and illustrations copyright © 2015 Neil Swaab

Book design by Neil Swaab and Chad W. Beckerman

Printed and bound in U.S.A.

10 9 8 7 6 5 4 3 2 1

THE ART OF BOOKS SINCE 1949

115 West 18th Street

New York, NY 10011

www.abramsbooks.com

To Bruce Swaab

CHAPTER ONE

Welcome to Middle School!

Gosh, it's nice to meet you! The name's Max Corrigan, and I'm the head of the Welcoming Committee here at William H. Taft. It's my job to help new kids like you adjust to this "dope" and "funky fresh" environment. I don't know if you've heard, but middle school is "way cool"! Do it right and it can be a "radical" experience where you'll make life-long pals, learn tons of interesting facts, and create the fondest memories a kid could dream of. Why, it might even be the best three years of your whole doggone life! And this packet contains everything you need to start your incredible journey!

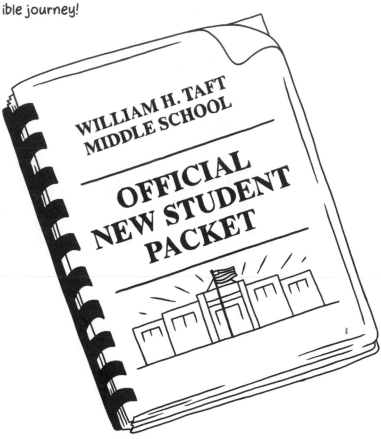

WILLIAM H. TAFT MIDDLE SCHOOL

OFFICIAL NEW STUDENT PACKET

Well, don't be a silly Billy, open it!

No, no, no, what I am is a *life coach*. I've helped kids all over this place, and I can show you, too, how to make middle school easier to beat than the first level of Candy Crush. Unfortunately, the Man doesn't approve of some of my more ... *unorthodox* methods, which is why I have to resort to this charade and advertise in secret. I'm not actually the head of the Welcoming Committee. In fact, this school doesn't even *have* a Welcoming Committee! Of course, the teachers here are so clueless, they don't even know that!

See what I mean? And these guys are supposed to be in charge of our future!

Anyway, you're lucky I got to you before it was too late. All that nice stuff I said about middle school before? Forget it. I don't want to exaggerate, but middle school is worse than getting a purple nurple on your you-know-what. You've got goons who are eight times bigger than you, teachers who love to make you suffer, and so many restrictions that even prisoners have more freedom. And if that's not bad enough, what happens in your first week will stick with you longer than the gum underneath your desk in homeroom. Blow it, and you could spend the next three years as lonely as Eugene Leach. He's such a scrub, even his imaginary friend's embarrassed to be seen with him.

As my client, you can be sure that won't happen. That's 'cuz I'll do whatever it takes to ensure your survival. And I mean *whatever*. I don't let silly things like rules or emotions or narrow views of right and wrong cloud my judgment. The way I see it, school life is hard, so you might as well make it as easy on yourself as possible. And—unlike certain competitors of mine named Kevin Carl—I know all there is to know about this place and have the perfect strategy to help you kick middle school's butt.

Want to hear it?

One word: cliques.

See, they're not just friends—cliques control the school. And getting accepted into one will give you all the protection you need.

But I would never settle for a *single* clique like my lesser peers—these days it's all about the crossover appeal. With my brilliant one-week plan, I intend to get you in with *all* of 'em! By the time your first five days are over, you won't just survive this place—you'll rule middle school like a boss!

Now, I will warn you in advance, there is a *slight* element of danger associated with my method. And Principal Sitz can be terrifying if he busts you for doing something wrong.

But you know that old saying: without risk, there's no reward. Besides, you only have five days before the Fall Assembly. And, as I mentioned before, first impressions are everything. If you haven't made a name for yourself by then, you might as well join Eugene's one-man pity party, 'cuz that's the closest you'll ever get to sitting at the cool kids' table. Or maybe that's what you want?

Did you at least get me a card?

Darndest thing: the invisible drugstore I went to was completely out of invisible birthday cards.

Yeah, I didn't think so.

So, come on. We'd better get down to business before it's too late. Step into my office and I'll tell you all about my epic plan.

CHAPTER TWO

The Epic Plan

I figure if you gotta work someplace, you might as well work where you get your best thinking done. Can I get you anything? An iced tea? Some OJ?

Toilet humor. Classic Lewis. He's my right-hand man. But I would never shake *his*, 'cuz he's always in the bathroom due to his irritable bowel syndrome.

So, let's get back to the Max Corrigan Foolproof Method of Success. There are a lot of cliques in this school you'll need to win over in order for this scheme to work. However, we can't go after *every* friend group, or you'll be here till the twelfth grade! That means we need to focus on the seven major ones.

First, you've got the Jocks. They're beloved throughout the school—especially during playoffs.

It's good to be king.

At the opposite end of the spectrum are the Nerds. I'm not just talking about some overachievers with good grades—these kids are so smart, some of 'em are already studying for the SATs.

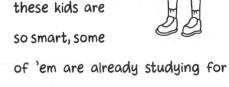

I'm learning Python—both the snake language **and** the programming language.

The Preps, on the other hand, can calculate the price of a pair of boat shoes in their heads faster than they can spend their parents' money. Designer clothes? Yacht club memberships? Spring break on the Amalfi Coast? If money can buy it, they've got it!

You can't put a price on class.

The Artists, though, will be starving for a while. That is, until they hit it big and get a show in a museum. These hipsters can do things

This piece of garbage? It's just a sketch.

with pencil and paper that even a blind man can see are totally amazeballs.

Speaking of "sensory impaired," you'd have to be deaf not to enjoy the Band Geeks. Sure, they might be on the lower end of the social ladder, but they stay alive through teamwork and strength in numbers.

Safety is music to our ears.

Not alive, naturally, would be *you* if you messed with the Tough Kids. Their reputation's as bad as Mr. Lipnicki's hairpiece. They bully, shoplift, and throw around words I've only seen in dark corners of the Internet after hacking the parental controls on my computer. These guys are no laughing matter.

Go $*@#
your %!&$ with
a #$&*, you
&$@%&!

If you like jokes, though, then the Class Clowns are your peeps. They keep school entertaining by disrupting boring classes, mocking teachers, and cracking us up with their sophisticated, cutting-edge brand of humor.

What's the difference between a large pizza and Mrs. Felcher? A large pizza's way less cheesy!

HA! HA! HA!

Since the Class Clowns are already kind of a laughingstock too, they're also the easiest clique to infiltrate. Which is why we're gonna start with them. And it just so happens that Randy "Tater Tot" Braverman—the most hilarious kid in the sixth grade—is in your first period. If you can impress him, the other Class Clowns will surely fall in line!

So, it's time we put this thing into gear and get to class. With my help, I'm positive Randy will greet you with all the respect you deserve.

CHAPTER THREE

Dying from Laughter

Or he could tear you apart and make you a target for every one of his jokes.

OK, I *may* have underestimated Randy a little bit—I forgot how much he loves going after noobs! And this is just his warm-up material! If he really gets on a roll, this could turn into a school-wide roast. Unless you do something fast, you'll become a punch line for every kid between here and the band room!

Your only hope is to dazzle him by cracking up the room with your most sidesplitting routine. And it better be killer! Like, Louis C.K. funny!

Don't worry if you don't know how to tell a joke, though. That's what you hired me for, remember? And I happen to have done a brief stint with the comedy troupe the Groundedlings in the fifth grade and can help. Pay attention, and I'll show you everything I know about weaving comedy gold:

HOW TO SLAY YOUR CLASS WITH A LEGENDARY COMIC ROUTINE

Any hack can get a cheap laugh by ripping a few juicy ones during a pop quiz. Being a true comedian, though, requires dedication, creativity, and an endless supply of "yo mama" jokes. Turn the page to learn how to do it.

KNOW YOUR STYLE

There are different types of class clownery. To stand out from the crowd, focus on the style you do best.

TYPES OF COMEDY

Observational

Why do they call it "homework"? I always do mine on the bus to school. Shouldn't they call it "buswork" instead?

Prop

I use this for the really **big** tests!

Impressionist

Here's my impression of Jeffrey McAllister at lunch yesterday:

What happened? Where's my pants?

You guys all know what I'm talkin' about!

Insult

Miss Applebaum is so strict, **Hitler** would have loved her! I mean, is this the third **period** or the Third **Reich**?

WORK ON YOUR TIMING

Knowing when it's OK and not OK to go for the big laugh is crucial.

OK

- In class
- At home
- Dance parties
- Whenever a teacher's back is turned
- Anytime someone splits their pants
- Holidays
- Field trips
- Lunch
- Whenever the planet Uranus is mentioned
- Bar mitzvahs
- Bat mitzvahs
- Anytime someone gets hit in the nuts
- Anytime someone falls down
- If there are monkeys around
- If a man has a funny-looking mustache
- If a woman has a funny-looking mustache
- At the mere mention of the word "poop"
- When you see a cat riding a dog

NOT OK

- Funerals (that's pretty much it)

TWO-DRINK MINIMUM

You know who doesn't want to laugh? Kids who are miserable and exhausted! Pump up your audience beforehand by plying them with tons of sugar. A couple cans of soda or some candy will make your routine seem like the illest ever!

CROWD WORK

Your material is just as important as your delivery. If you're stumped on what to joke about, look to your teachers or other authority figures! A secretary who's obsessed with troll dolls or a teacher with a really bad comb-over can be a comedy gold mine! Talk to your audience and see if there's anything funny from them that you can use in your set.

USE YOUR SURROUNDINGS

People aren't the only thing you can mine for jokes. A good location can provide a wealth of material. For instance, a class field trip to an unexpected place can be a comedy bonanza!

CONSIDER YOUR WORD CHOICE

Some words are just funnier than others! *Underwear* is lame, but *tighty-whities* really paints a picture. And why say "butt" when you can say "stink station"? Always think about word choice when constructing your jokes. And don't be afraid to use "colorful" language for emphasis! (See the sidebar on page 26 to learn more!)

DULLSVILLE

> Mr. Chu is such a jerk. Everyone hates him.

HILARIOUS

> Mr. Chu is such a tool, the janitor could use him to unclog toilets!

$#&!

WORKING BLUE

Sometimes swearing just makes things funnier! In comedy, that's called "working blue." If you need to add a little zip to your jokes, give it a try! Sure, you might get sent to the principal's office, but do you really want to live in a world where you can't say "*&@^" or "!$%&"?

> *!$%, no!

PRACTICE MAKES PERFECT

Finally, refine your material. Practice your bits first in the classroom before dropping them in the auditorium. Then, when you perform for the masses, you know your set will kill!

OK, I've warmed you up as best I can. Now hit the class with your funniest six minutes. I just hope you kill it out there. Otherwise, Randy's jokes could kill you!

CHAPTER FOUR

A FUNNY THING HAPPENED

Somebody get a doctor, 'cuz I just busted a gut!

I TAKE EVERYTHING BACK! I HAVEN'T LAUGHED THAT HARD SINCE MR. BASSETT'S PANTS CAUGHT ON FIRE WHEN HE WAS SHOWING US THOSE BUNSEN BURNERS! AND YOUR ARMPIT NOISES? I COULD HAVE SWORN I WAS LISTENING TO THE REAL THING! SERIOUSLY, I COULD ALMOST SMELL THE FARTS!

LOOK, I'M GONNA BE HONEST. I'D LOVE FOR YOU TO HANG WITH THE **CLASS CLOWNS** AND OPEN FOR ME IN SOME OF MY CLASSES. UNFORTUNATELY, THOSE SLOTS—MUCH LIKE MY BABY BROTHER'S DIAPERS—ARE CONSTANTLY FULL.

STILL, I MIGHT BE ABLE TO WORK SOMETHING OUT IF YOU CAN HELP ME WITH A MAJOR PROBLEM.

WHILE MY FELLOW COMEDIANS' JOKES ARE KILLER, THEIR DRAWING ABILITY IS AS BAD AS MR. LAMBERT'S MORNING COFFEE BREATH. I MEAN, CHECK THIS OUT!

HERE'S THE THING: SUBMISSIONS FOR THE SCHOOL NEWS-PAPER ARE NEXT WEEK! IF OUR COMIC STRIPS ARE GONNA HAVE ANY CHANCE OF GETTING IN, WE NEED PEOPLE WHO CAN DRAW.

OTHERWISE, WE'RE GONNA END UP WITH ANOTHER YEAR'S WORTH OF HELPER HARRY CARTOONS!

IF YOU CAN TEAM UP MY WRITERS WITH PEOPLE WHO CAN ACTUALLY HOLD A PEN, I'LL LET YOU INTO MY CREW AND TAKE YOU ON TOUR WITH ME. HECK, YOU OPEN FOR ME LONG ENOUGH, YOU MIGHT EVEN GET TO HEADLINE YOUR *OWN* CLASSES.

SO, WHAT DO YOU SAY? MAKE THIS HAPPEN AND I PREDICT YOU'LL HAVE A FUTURE THAT'S NOTHING BUT FUNNY BUSINESS.

CHAPTER FIVE

Sketchy Characters

Wow, that went better than I expected! But let's not celebrate just yet. We still have a long way to go.

Speaking of which, we'd better get back to work, 'cuz now we've got to find some kids who can draw the Class Clowns' comic strips. But who do we know who can wield a marker like a ninja?

I know! The Artists! If anyone can bring the Class Clowns' jokes to life, it's them!

Sadly, getting in with these hipsters isn't as easy as completing a paint-by-number. The Artists are all about being unique and won't listen to just anyone.

To convince them to help and let you join their collective, you'll need to win over their leader, Eraser Head, the sickest Artist at William H. Taft Middle School. His graffiti's been exhibited in the most prestigious places around, including the boys' bathroom, under the bleachers, and the side of the school. He's dope!

There's one major problem, though: nobody knows who Eraser Head really is. He's kept his identity secret to avoid being caught by Principal Sitz.

The only way to "draw" him out is to create a piece of art so insane, it'll blow the entire school away. Unfortunately, I don't know about you, but I scribble worse than a blind man with no arms and an uncontrollable tic. I mean, one time I tried to draw an orange and it came out looking like this:

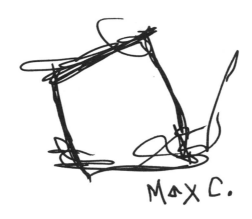

Max C.

Not to worry, though. While I can't teach you how to make a masterpiece, I *can* teach you how to pass your work off as one. So grab your pens and paper, 'cuz I'm gonna show you

HOW TO CONVINCE PEOPLE YOU'RE AN ARTISTIC GENIUS EVEN IF YOU CAN BARELY HOLD A PENCIL

Talent isn't the only way to get ahead in the art world. With a little bit of cunning, lies, and shameless promotion, you too can be middle school's next Van Gogh! Here's how.

GOOD ARTISTS COPY, GREAT ARTISTS STEAL

Why waste all that time, sweat, and energy learning how to draw when you can simply pass something off as your own? Go onto the Internet, find a painting that no one else would recognize, and then print it out on watercolor or canvas paper! They'll never be able to tell it's not the real thing!

THE MEDIUM IS THE MESSAGE

You can create art out of *anything*! In fact, you can even make it out of *nothing at all*! Just go about your regular day like always, but tell everyone it's performance art!

GIVE YOUR WORK A RIDICULOUS TITLE TO MAKE IT SOUND WAY MORE IMPORTANT

A good title can elevate a cruddy drawing into a master-work! Fool kids into thinking it's deep by picking the most nonsensical title you can think of. The longer and crazier, the better!

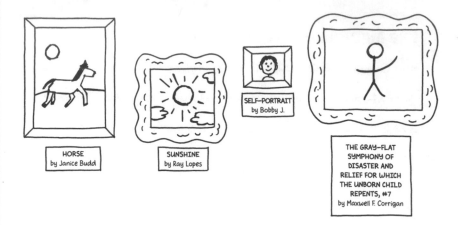

HORSE
by Janice Budd

SUNSHINE
by Ray Lopes

SELF-PORTRAIT
by Bobby J.

THE GRAY-FLAT
SYMPHONY OF
DISASTER AND
RELIEF FOR WHICH
THE UNBORN CHILD
REPENTS, #7
by Maxwell F. Corrigan

TALK THE TALK

When you talk about your art, make sure to use a lot of big words so your work seems deeper than it really is. And give the pieces super-meaningful explanations too! The dumber you can make people feel, the smarter your work will appear! For inspiration, see the sidebar on page 38.

CREATE SOME BUZZ

Finally, the most important thing you can do is get influential people to vouch for your art. So get it in front of them by any means necessary. 'Cuz if a bunch of important kids say it's good, a lot of other ones will like it too, no matter how much it stinks! I mean, look at Picasso! The folks in his paintings have, like, six noses and yet everyone says he's a *genius!*

What We Talk About When We Talk About Art

Need to convince people your art's the bomb? Here's a list of random buzzwords you can throw in at any time that will make people think you're a true artistic visionary! Don't worry if you don't know what they mean—most other people won't either!

- Juxtaposition
- Intrinsic value
- Appropriation
- Boundaries
- Enigmatic

- Objectification
- Probing
- Curation
- The Other
- Postmodern

- Prolific
- Aesthetics
- Provoke
- Ambiguous
- The Gaze

All right, here's some paper, a glue stick, a few crayons, a dead bird's foot, a book of old Norse poetry found in an insane asylum, and a flattened penny. Make me a masterpiece!

I'm really digging your use of the bird's foot here.

Wow, that was fast! And let me say, that is one truly . . . *interesting* piece of art you just created! Great art provokes a response, and yours is certainly doing that! I think the school's even considering it for its permanent collection!

But, more than anything, you caught Eraser Head's attention. Or haven't you noticed your locker?

You'd better get up there soon! And don't blow it! You only get one shot with a guy like him!

CHAPTER SIX

Artistic Statement

Figures. People are always misjudging me and my work. But that's OK; it keeps my identity secret. Yours certainly isn't, though.

Your art's gotten a lot of acclaim in such a short time. And I have to admit, it's not bad. It's almost as if you're trying to defy our notions of what art really is. Bravo.

So, word on the street is you need my assistance with some comic strips. Well, I have to be honest, that's not really my thing. What I do is social commentary for the masses, not a bunch of cheap jokes for the school paper.

However, I wonder if there's a way we can both benefit from this?

See, I just found the perfect spot for my next piece of art that's going to take it to a whole new level. Literally. It's on the highest wall of the cafeteria, above the vending machines. But there's no way I can complete it while the place is so busy at lunch.

Look, you're good at getting people's attention. So maybe you can help me?

If you can find a way to distract everyone long enough for me to finish my masterpiece, I'll convince the Artists to lend their skills to the Class Clowns. I might also be willing to let you roll with us, and we could give your work the exposure it really needs.

What do you say?

CHAPTER SEVEN

The Hot Seat

I can't believe you got to meet Eraser Head! What was he like? I bet he was a really cool guy with, like, an eye patch and a giant scar.

So, he said we've got to create a distraction in the cafeteria for him, huh? I know just the thing: a massive food fight! It's perfect, except for one problem: the Band Geeks!

See, the Band Geeks sit right next to where Eraser Head wants to make his art. And they'd never move from their seats during lunch. Not even if there was a food fight of epic proportion. That's 'cuz their table is prime real estate—right by the soda machines.

In order to get them out of their chairs, you'd have to be seated with them as part of their crew. And the only way to do that is to go through their band leader, Cleavon Mitchell, the baddest middle schooler to ever sling a sax.

Go, Cleavon!

Feel it, my man!

That's one fine groove, daddy-o.

Unfortunately, Cleavon doesn't let just *anyone* sit at his table. In fact, *no one* in middle school does, 'cuz where you sit at lunch is *everything*. And *every* group is represented in the lunchroom. If you don't believe me, look around!

And that's just *one side* of the cafeteria!

This is gonna take some major finesse. Luckily for you, I've got more than enough swag to spare. Why, there isn't a table in this place I *can't* chow down with. Even the lunch ladies know I'm legit.

So get your tray and follow me. I'm gonna give you the 411 on . . .

HOW TO FIND A LUNCH CREW WITHOUT TOTALLY EATING IT

Securing a lunch table is one of the most stressful things a middle schooler can do. Ace it, and lunchtime will be the best part of your day. Blow it, and you could wind up with a permanent ulcer from the constant anxiety. Here are my tips:

SCOPE OUT THE AREA

There are a lot of tables to sit at. Before you panic and head for any old one, take a minute to get the lay of the land. If you're a beginner, try to go with a table that seems open to noobs.

DRESS TO IMPRESS

When you've found a table you want to sit at, check yourself first. Middle schoolers are some of the harshest critics on the planet, so you need to bring your A game. Ask yourself the following questions before proceeding:

LUNCHROOM CHECKLIST

☑ **Have I played twelve games of basketball in the past two days and *not* showered?**

☑ **Is my lunch so gross that other kids might pass out just from seeing it?**

☑ **Is my fly down?**

☑ **Am I naked?**

☑ **Is there a massive piece of spinach stuck between my front teeth (from the night before, no less!)?**

☑ **Would *I* be embarrassed to sit with me?**

☑ **Am I secretly an alien who's going to suck out everyone's brains so I can mind-control the entire school?**

☑ **Am I currently crying from fear?**

If you answered "yes" to any of these questions, STOP! Take a minute to fix everything until you're as presentable as possible. And then go ahead. (And, by the way, if you're secretly an alien, I'm on to you. I just want you to know that.)

INTRODUCE YOURSELF

When you get to the table, play it nice and cool. Go up to the group and say hi. If you know something about any of the kids, give 'em a quick compliment. Something like, "Nice answers in math class. Boy, you're pretty smart!" or, "Hey, aren't you the kid who likes blowing up textbooks with cherry bombs? Man, you really got some distance on that last one." That should warm the table up. Then introduce yourself and, really casually, like it's no big deal, ask if you can sit with them. Like so:

Mind if I crash with you guys for a bit? This seems like a cool spot.

BRIBE THEM IF YOU HAVE TO

If they tell you to get lost, you might have to resort to bribery. That's why I always carry extra junk food and comic books around. You'd be surprised what that can buy in a jam.

Aw, that's too bad. 'Cuz I got all these extra Kit Kat bars but no one to share them with.

Uh, did I say "No way?" I meant "No way are you sitting anywhere **else**!"

RESPECT THE TABLE

Once seated, remember that you're a guest. Don't monopolize the conversation or blather on endlessly about yourself. Share your food. Get to know your tablemates. Ask some questions to find out about them. Here are some classic icebreakers I always use:

MAX CORRIGAN'S
TOP 10 GET-TO-KNOW-YOU QUESTIONS

- Do you have any brothers or sisters?

- Which teacher, would you say, sucks the most?

- What class do you have first period?

- Would you rather be able to fly or be invisible?

- Who's the best Michael: Michael Jackson, Michael Jordan, or Michelangelo? (Will accept either the painter or the Ninja Turtle.)

- If you were strandod on a desert island with only one person, would you kill and eat them if you had to?

- If you could pick any five people in all of history to eat lunch with, who would they be? Sub-question: what are you eating?

- Cats versus dogs: where do you stand?

- What's your favorite TV show?

- What's the most number of times you've vomited in one day?

Don't stress if none of these questions works. You can always try some of my amazing conversation starters too. (See the sidebar on the facing page.)

BE YOURSELF. OR NOT.

Finally, when you do get comfortable, just relax and be yourself. I'm sure they'll like you for you—although if they don't, you should pretend to be someone else. Here's a trick I always use when I'm in a tight corner: I imagine what somebody cooler/smarter/funnier might do, and then I just do *that* instead! It works every time!

Don't know how to break the ice? These

AMAZING CONVERSATION STARTERS

will make you the kid *everyone* wants to talk to!

- "I can tell you're the kind of guy who really appreciates a good fire."

- "Homework. *Pshh.* Am I right?"

- "Check out this awesome scab on my _____!" (only works with boys)

- "I know this place where you can see a dead body."

- "I don't suppose you know anyone who wants some video games? I have *way more* than I could ever play."

- "Can you direct me to the library so I can study? Nah, just kidding; I'm headed to the principal's office. I got into trouble for being too *awesome*."

- "You have *not lived* until you've seen the mess someone just left in the boys' bathroom."

CONVERSATION STARTERS TO AVOID

"Is anyone else here a fan of ventriloquism?"

"I've been itching to talk to you. And not just because of my rash."

"Check out this awesome scab on my _____!" (to girls)

"I've got tons of liver pâté! Who's in?"

"Please like me! Please!"

OK, it's up to you now. I don't want to freak you out or anything, but if you blow this, you could end up eating "Mommy's lunches" in the bathroom stall next to Lewis for the next couple of months! Or, *worse*, sitting at Eugene's table.

So go over to Cleavon and introduce yourself. And remember, be likable!

CHAPTER EIGHT

The Right Notes

I dig your vibe. Usually, we never warm up to new kids, but I could see you chillin' on some of our jam sessions. Yeah, I feel it. But I have to admit, this food-fighting bag of yours? That's not our scene.

See, we're all about bringin' the love. Also, the Coke machine's right here, and right now it's practically the only thing we got. 'Cuz I don't know if you heard, but things are starting to look pretty gloomy for us.

See, the school's thinking of cutting band class. And that's a major bummer. So, we've got to sell all these candy bars to raise money for the program. Problem is, the football team needs new equipment too, and they're out there competing with us! And, wouldn't you know, people would rather buy from those squares than from us. If we don't make some major sales soon, we're doomed!

However . . .

Maybe we can strike a deal?

You seem like a person who can get things done. If you can figure out a way to shut those guys down so we can sell our stock, I'd be happy to give up the Coke machine. We would also have a permanent spot for you here at our table. We could jam every day.

So, how 'bout it? Do this for me, and you'll be in the mix. Clam it up, and your demise will be music to my ears.

Feel me?

CHAPTER NINE

Unfriendly Competition

Nicely done! See, I knew you'd be a hit with the Band Geeks! And while you were rapping with Cleavon, I managed to use my sweet bartering skills to trade my stupid healthy turkey sandwich for *fifteen chocolate puddings!*

What? I'm not addicted—I can quit any time I want. I just don't want to, OK, so get off my back.

Anyway, I'm proud of you! It looks like you're really picking up on this whole "middle school" thing. Yeah, if you keep this up, I don't think there's a single thing that can get in your way.

I may have spoken too soon. That walking headache is Freddy Dugan. He's a new student too. Unlike you, though, he's the biggest jerk this school's ever seen! I mean, the kid is more bad news than the school newspaper. And they print the *lunch menu!*

Ha-ha! Looks like someone peed their pants!

What the—! And he seemed like such a good kid when I met him too. I don't know what could have possibly turned him into a complete psycho overnight.

Of course! Kevin Carl! My nemesis!

I should have figured! Kevin Carl used to be my protégé. I took him under my wing when he first got here. Showed him everything I know. We were partners, committed to changing the lives of middle schoolers everywhere together.

But then he suddenly took all my information and started his own competing business! He poached my clients! Ran attack ads all over school! Sabotaged me at every turn! He's the most depraved human being I've ever known. That's why I always say: never trust a guy with two first names!

See what I mean? What kind of sick mind would think of that?

We've got to do something fast or else you'll be the laughingstock of the entire cafeteria!

I know! My last pudding cup!

Quickly, smash it on Freddy's butt! No time for questions! Just do it!

Now run! Fast! Before they have time to retaliate!

Whew! That was close!

But at least you're in the clear. And I think everything's going to be OK now that you're finally—

My office. **Now!**

Uh-oh.

Chapter Ten

THE PRINCIPAL'S PRINCIPLES

I've seen your type before. Blatant disregard for the rules. A rebel. Think you can get something over on this place. Well, here's a news flash: out of all the kids who try stuff, it always ends the same way—badly.

Delinquency will not flourish in these halls. Especially this close to the Fall Assembly. It's my most important assembly of the year, and I won't see it ruined by punks like you terrorizing upstanding students like Kevin Carl and his friend Freddy. Kevin's an exemplary member of this school, and you should strive to be more like him.

Since this pudding incident is your first offense, I'm letting you off with a warning. But don't think you've gotten away with anything. I've got my eye on you now, and I'll be watching you like a hawk with binoculars inside a telescope. If I get a *whiff* of even one more infraction, you'll feel the full weight of my power. Understood?

Oh, and one last thing: your buddy Max? He's trouble, and anyone who listens to him will find themselves in a lot more of it. Don't trust anything he says.

Now straighten up and fly right. Otherwise, I'll show you just how unpleasant middle school can really be.

Have I made myself clear?

CHAPTER ELEVEN

The Haves and the Have-Nots

Oh man, I'm sorry about that. I barely got out unscathed *myself*! I'm telling you, Principal Sitz is the *worst*. I've had charley horses that were less painful than spending a minute in his office. I swear, the guy won't be happy until the entire school is filled with obedient, mind-controlled robots who never question anything. And he's totally got it in for me and my clients, while he thinks Kevin's a golden boy. As if! One of these days, though, I'm gonna finally stand up to him and prove him wrong. Really!

Why are you looking at me so funny? He didn't say anything to you about me, did he? You sure? OK, good. 'Cuz we can't lose focus. If you keep your eyes on the prize and keep doing what you're doing, you might even get on the radar of Darnell Dalton and Caitlin Wilkes, the most popular kids in the sixth grade! They're so influential, they're practically celebrities!

Of course, that's a long way to go. And now—with Freddy Dugan and Kevin Carl after you, and Principal Sitz breathing down your neck—even getting through the day's gonna be a lot harder than I thought. We'll need to double our efforts. That means we simply have to get all those chocolate bars from the football team off the streets to appease Cleavon Mitchell and the Band Geeks.

Unfortunately, I haven't figured out a way to do that just yet. Not only do you need to get rid of the chocolate bars, but you have to do it in such a way that you won't cost the football team their new gear! Trust me, you do *not* want to be the team's enemy. Rumor has it, if you listen carefully at night, you can still hear the screams on the twenty-yard line of the last kid who crossed them.

Hmm . . . This is gonna require some serious thought.

Tell you what, why don't we regroup in the morning so I can devote all my energy to this? Hopefully by then I'll have found an answer to all your problems.

TUESDAY

CHAPTER TWELVE

At Any Cost

Sorry, I must have dozed off! I spent the entire night brainstorming and plotting how to solve this dilemma. Lewis was up all night too.

So, I think I finally found some good solutions to getting all those chocolate bars off the streets. Check it: we could disguise ourselves as ninjas and break into the locker rooms under the cover of darkness and steal the bars right from under the Jocks' noses! *Or* we could focus on building up our telepathic powers until they're so great that we can mentally control the Jocks and get them to dump the whole lot into the river without them even realizing what they've done! *Or* we could create a human-rhinoceros hybrid who terrorizes the school and the only thing that can bring it down is sweet, sweet sugar from the Jocks. Although, come to think of it, I don't have much ninja training; it would take decades just to learn how to read minds, let alone control them; and I'd never be able to get access to enough rhinoceros DNA or an advanced flow cytometry unit. Plus my dad's always yelling at me about playing God.

I guess we could just buy all the chocolate if we needed to?

That's it! We'll get rid of Cleavon Mitchell's competition *and* fund the football team. We get to be heroes, and we can sell everything back at marked-up prices down the road for a nice, tidy profit! Awesome, right?

Problem is, it would cost a *lot* of money up front to buy all the chocolate bars from the Jocks. And we don't have anywhere close to the money we'd need.

But maybe we don't have to use our own cash.

What if we found some investors to front the dough instead? You know, give out a loan in exchange for a cut of the profits?

But who can we think of who has that much wealth?

I know! No one has more cash than the Preps. And the richest one of all is Elana Bender. Her parents are loaded! If she likes your style, you've got it made! Easy-peasy, right?

I wish.

Unfortunately, Elana is the biggest tightwad this school's ever seen. She never parts with her money unless she can be assured she'll get it back. And if you're not already raking in the dough? Good luck!

To convince Elana to make it rain, you'll have to fool her into thinking you're already wealthy. That means she can't see you looking all busted. You've got to sport the newest brand-name clothes and flash a wad of dough an inch thick. And that's gonna cost a pretty penny in and of itself.

As luck would have it, though, I can help. I happen to have taken a few correspondence courses in personal finance, and I consider myself to be kind of an expert. Follow my lead and I'll show you . . .

HOW TO TURN MIDDLE SCHOOL INTO YOUR OWN PERSONAL ATM

There's a sucker born every minute. And their money should be rightfully yours. If you know how to wheel and deal, you can make a small fortune in middle school! Here's how:

AUCTION YOUR STUFF

You know all your old, useless junk you never use? Why not give that sentimental value some *real* value and sell it off in an auction? To maximize your profit, have a friend make fake bids on your items to drive the prices up! If for some reason he wins an item, he can just give it back to you after it's over and no one will be the wiser!

BUY FOR A DOLLAR, SELL FOR TWO

Things are a lot cheaper when they're bought in bulk. So, buy a whole box of whatever's in demand, then unload the items individually to other students for higher prices when kids need them the most! That's some good profit!

"DISCOUNT" SALES

This is the biggest scam in retail. Mark up your prices beforehand. Then declare a huge limited-time sale and bring the items back down to their original pre-marked-up prices! Kids will be so excited by the "discount," they'll snap them up like crazy without even noticing that your sale stuff is the same price as your regular stuff was!

DONATIONS

If selling things isn't your style, consider asking for donations. Everyone loves to support a good cause, so creating a fake one or pretending to have an affliction can serve you quite well!

OUTSOURCING

Here's a great scam: let somebody hire you for a job. Then, instead of doing the job yourself, pay another kid less money to do it for you, and keep the difference! Do this with twenty or thirty jobs and you've got yourself a nice business without having to do any of the actual work!

HAVE CONFIDENCE

A good confidence man—or con man—can clear a ton of money in a very short time. All you have to do is set up a scam, gain your target's trust, and then make off with their money before they even know what's happening! (See the sidebar on page 81 for my favorite example.)

WHAT YOU'LL NEED:

A good disguise.

Ability to remain cool under pressure.

A getaway.

The name's Maximus Corningwall, and my boss—a Nigerian prince—needs your help.

THE RARE COMIC BOOK

1. Wear a disguise so you can't be recognized.

2. Find a "mark." This is a dim-witted kid with money who you can easily trick.

3. Tell your mark that you need his help to pay off a bully who stole your rare comic book. It's worth a fortune, but the bully doesn't know that. In exchange for the mark's help, when the comic's returned, you'll give him an even greater sum of money than he gave you, as a thank-you gift.

4. Here's where the con comes in: there is no actual comic book! It's all made up! Once you've got the money, run like the wind!

5. Change out of your disguise and the mark will never be able to find you or get his money back.

Nicely done! Keep doing what you're doing and I think you could be up there with the business greats like Charles Ponzi and Bernie Madoff! And now that you look like a hundred-aire, there's no way Elana Bender will refuse to fund your exciting business venture. I'm 100 percent positive it will be a smashing success!

CHAPTER THIRTEEN

A Class Act

The thing is, I don't like chocolate. I'm a vanilla girl. And I have to be excited about something in order to sink my money in it.

Still, I like your hustle. And I like to invest in people. And you're clearly a kid who knows about wealth.

I have a counteroffer I'd like to propose.

While I may be a gambler, you know what I love even more? A sure thing. There's an underground betting ring in school, and I'd like to rig it in my favor by convincing the football team to take a dive in their next game.

Of course, as you can imagine, that's easier said than done. Every time I suggest it, let's just say the response has been . . . *less than positive*. However, you might have more success.

If you can talk some sense into those muscle heads, I'll be happy to loan you all the cash you need. And I'll even let my other friends know that you're top dollar. You can hang with us and experience middle school the way it was meant to be—in first class.

Naturally, if you don't want to, I'll be just as happy to use my vast funds to keep you in coach until you graduate. You'll be lucky if you ever see another dime the rest of the time you're here.

So, what do you think? Are you ready to go into business together and make a fortune? Because I think you and I could make great partners.

CHAPTER FOURTEEN
Muscle-Bound

I'm not so sure about this. If there's one clique you don't mess with, it's the Jocks. To even bring up throwing a game to them would be instant suicide. Like, *buried-underneath-the-bleachers-in-a-shallow-grave-where-no-one-will-ever-find-you-again* dead.

However, you'll also go belly-up if you *don't* go through with this. So I guess you don't have much of a choice.

In order for this to work, you're gonna need to gain the Jocks' trust. That means you'll need to think like a Jock. And act like a Jock. And play like a Jock. C'mon, it's time for gym class anyway. I'm sure we can pass you off as one of their own!

Yeah, you're screwed.

Look, I'm sorry, but do you have any idea who that kid is? That amazing specimen is Tiger Sylvester, the greatest athlete the school's ever seen! He's so incredible, he once scored a touchdown in a baseball game! There's no way you can rise to his level!

New kid! Quit lollygagging and get your butt out here! We're doing power squats next!

Oh God! One step onto that gym floor and Tiger will instantly recognize you for the puddle of soggy muscles you really are. It's all gonna be over!

Wait. Maybe you *shouldn't* step foot on the gym floor. I mean, if Tiger never sees you in action, there's no way he could know you're *not* a Jock, right? You know, so long as you keep up appearances?

OK, we only have a few seconds, so pay attention! Follow my workout routine, and I'll make sure you're benched permanently!

HOW TO GET OUT OF GYM CLASS WITHOUT BREAKING A SWEAT

FEEL THE BURN

Pretending you're under the weather is a slam dunk toward getting yourself excused for the day. It's a gym classic. Now drop and give me fifty "I don't feel well all of a sudden"s!

NO PAIN, NO GAIN

If you want more time off, you could always fake an injury. A few bucks spent wisely at the medical supply store can be an absolute lifesaver. Now give me twelve "ankle sprains," stat!

THE KID GLOVES ARE OFF

"Forgetting" your gym clothes can buy you a well-deserved day off when you need it most (though it might count against your grade). Just make sure your teacher doesn't have a backup, or you could face wearing the dreaded spare!

Now give me ten "clothes hiders," and make 'em good!

The
BROMANCE LANGUAGES

Need to communicate with Jocks but don't know your end-arounds from your power sweeps? Fake it by repeating these generic phrases:

- "Did you see that incredible play last night, bruh?"

- "So, my mom hid my protein powder 'cuz she said it wasn't good for me or something, but I was like, 'Whoa, brah, I'm just tryna get big, why you gotta shut me down like that?' You feel me, bro?"

- "You pumped for the game this week?"

- "I'm totally off carbs now. That stuff is whack. Now I'm gonna get a six-pack. By the time summer comes, I'ma be ripped."

- "Can you believe that terrible call yesterday? Is the ref blind or something?"

- "I can't decide which workout to do after school: P90X, Insanity, or Asylum. Eh, I guess I'll just do 'em all."

- "I just think the team was better five years ago."

- "It's all about conditioning, bruh. Conditioning."

WORK ON YOUR REPS

Your reputation, that is! If you're known for being a men-
ace on the field, no gym teacher in their right mind will let
you anywhere near a high-impact activity.

OK, quick! Get your game face on and suit up! I've
coached you well. There's no doubt in my mind you'll get out
of gym class and Tiger will be your new best bro!

CHAPTER FIFTEEN

TIGER'S ROAR

I don't care how good at sports you say you are, no self-respecting athlete would ever suggest throwing a game! I mean, seriously, what kind of gutless, conniving, moral-less scrub would even consider that? You must think you're pretty smart, huh?

Well? Answer me! Do you?

For real.
Do you think
you're smart?

Look, I'm sorry for Hulking out. It's just that, well, I'm going through some real drama at the moment.

See, even if I wanted to, I couldn't convince my team to throw the game this week. That's 'cuz I may not even *be* a part of the team anymore. My parents say if I don't get my test scores up, I'll have to give up football and focus on my studies permanently. And football's my life!

But I'll tell you what. Maybe you can do something for me. You seem like a smart kid. If you promise to improve my grades, I might be able to help you out. I mean, without me, the team is guaranteed to lose the season anyway. But if I'm in and we just throw a single game? One loss won't be the end of the world. And I'd be so grateful, I'd even let you fetch water for us or something while we play. You could be an honorary team member.

So, how about it? Fix my problems and we'll take it easier on the field for our next game. Fail, though? And the team will be using *you* as a practice dummy.

We good?

CHAPTER SIXTEEN

Socially Awkward

OMG, you're alive! Wow! For a minute there, I thought Tiger was gonna beat you into oblivion! But you did it! That was legendary! You certainly have some good survival instincts. I'm gaining a whole new respect for you, and I'm sure everyone else in this school must be too!

I wonder what bug crawled up their butts? Seriously. I don't think you've done anything *that bad* since you've been here. I should tweet about it, 'cuz—

Have you checked your social media yet today? OK, well, *don't!* Let's just say someone posted a lot of vicious lies about you and certain toilets you may or may not have clogged after third period. It's, uh, it's pretty scandalous stuff.

Freddy Dugan and Kevin Carl! I should've known!

Oh man! If this keeps up, your rep's gonna be shredded!

This is major trouble!

Ugh. Just when things were going so well.

CHAPTER SEVENTEEN

Over the Moon

I thought things were bad before, but now they're nuclear! We've only got three more days. If we don't get these cliques on your side by then, Freddy Dugan and Kevin Carl are going to make you a bigger outcast than Eugene Leach! And even *I* can't help you when you've fallen as far as him!

So, now instead of doubling our efforts, we need to quadruple them! No, scratch that. We need to do two times *more* than a quadruple! What is that—an *octoduple?* That can't be a word, can it? Anyway, what I'm saying is, we've gotta step up our game.

Speaking of which, the William H. Taft Herons need to lose their next one for you to succeed. That means Tiger Sylvester's test scores have gotta make a comeback more dramatic than the team's last match against the North Lathrup Eagles.

As brilliant as I am, I'm not genius enough to work a miracle like that. This would take someone truly brainy. If only we knew someone smart enough to tutor him . . .

Wait! Are you thinking what I'm thinking?

Of course! Rufus the Janitor!

He knows all kinds of weird, useful things! I mean, he once helped me concoct a fake-vomit recipe that I *still* use to this day.

Oh, you were thinking of someone else? Who?

The Nerds?

Well, that's even better!

And the smartest one of all is Dallas Foster. He's eight years old and *already* in the seventh grade. The kid's a prodigy. Or didn't you read his interview in the school paper this morning?

The William H. Taft Tattler

DALLAS FOSTER: NERD WITH A VISION

Why his new app will change everything we know about middle school . . .

SERIAL WEDGIE-ER TIGHTENS GRIP ON BUMMED-OUT MIDDLE SCHOOL!

HERONS PREP FOR THE NEXT BIG GAME! HUGE EXPECTATIONS FOR A WIN!

HELPER HARRY

WHY DOES IT FEEL LIKE I BOUGHT THIS GRADE?

BECAUSE YOU *PAID* ATTENTION IN CLASS! AND HERE'S YOUR CHANGE!

If we can get him to help Tiger, you'll be home free!

Problem is, not only have the Jocks made the Nerds' lives miserable, but Dallas won't even talk to you unless you've got some grade-A Nerd clout. And that's not easy to come by.

However, what if you had something that could grant you instant Nerd approval? Something that was so awesome all the Nerds in school would fog up their glasses over it? Like some kind of amazing Nerd memorabilia?

What have you got in your pockets?

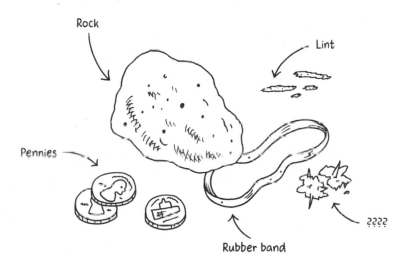

OK, that's not great. But maybe it doesn't *have* to be great—just so long as the Nerds *think* it is. That rock, for instance! What if it wasn't just an ordinary schoolyard rock? What if it was, say, a *moon rock?*

Hey, it could be true! And once we convince the Nerds of it, there'll be a line longer than an Apple Store on the day of the new iPhone release to talk to you. And I know exactly how we can fool 'em:

HOW TO FOOL PEOPLE INTO THINKING YOUR WORTHLESS PIECE OF JUNK IS A RARE COLLECTIBLE

Any hunk of garbage can be turned into a priceless antique. All it takes is some research, a little bit of storytelling, and a few scraps of evidence to win over the harshest skeptics. Here's my guide:

KNOW YOUR STUFF

In order to seem like you know what you're talking about, you have to . . . well . . . *know what you're talking about.*

That means learning all the right dates, locations, and people involved. If you seem like an expert, people will think your fake collectible is that much more credible.

CREATE A BACKSTORY

This insanely rare object had to come to you *somehow*! For anyone to believe it's real, you have to have a really good story for how you got it. If possible, connect it with the original owner. It will make your "collectible" even more doubt-proof.

HAVE SOME SUPPORTING ITEMS TO GO WITH IT

For extra authenticity, find some other stuff to support your fake rarity. Things that wouldn't be as priceless as the object, but would still be pretty cool and help sell it. It could be something as simple as a fake autograph (see the sidebar on page 109) or just some extra junk that you can tell a few good lies about.

GENERATE A CERTIFICATE OF AUTHENTICITY

Finally, nothing says "authentic" like a certificate of authenticity. Fortunately, anybody can make one. Just design one on the computer or download a template and print it out on really old paper (or fake a paper's age by crinkling it and soaking it in coffee, tea, or dark soda). Use a lot of official-sounding words and old typewriter fonts and frame it so it looks like it's been in your family for generations. Like so:

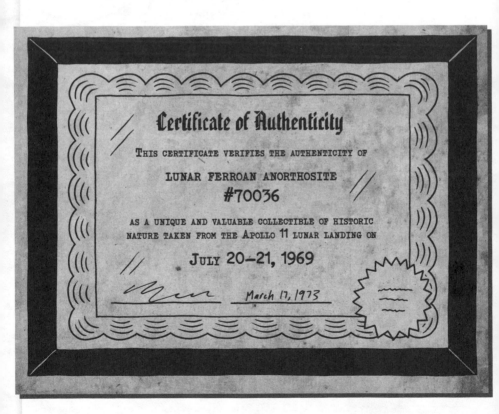

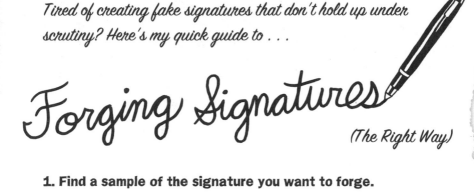

Tired of creating fake signatures that don't hold up under scrutiny? Here's my quick guide to . . .

Forging Signatures
(The Right Way)

1. Find a sample of the signature you want to forge.

2. Analyze it. Look for any distinct letters or properties that make it unique or identifiable. Maybe it has a weird squiggly *n*, or a heart over the lowercase *i*, or it slants to the left instead of the right. Note all of those telltale characteristics and commit them to memory.

3. Get some tracing paper.

4. Trace over the signature, making sure to capture the unique properties from step #2. At first, yours won't look that great. That's OK.

5. Keep repeating step #4 over and over again until the strokes become second nature to you. Go faster each time. This may take a while.

6. After you've finally mastered it, try it without the tracing paper. Compare against the original, especially noting the more distinct letterforms. Repeat until they look identical.

7. When you're ready to actually sign, use the same kind of pen and paper the person you're forging would use. That way, it should match exactly and no one will be the wiser!

Wow, if I didn't know it was fake, I'd swear that rock you're holding was not of this earth! You've really got everyone fooled—the entire Nerdosphere is abuzz! And now there's no way Dallas can resist the temptation to talk to you. As soon as we find him, we can—

Hold on. Someone's approaching! It's not Dallas, though! Who is that?

Ahhhhh!!!! It's a ghost!

Run! Run!

R-U-U-U-U-U-N-N-N-N!!!!!!

CHAPTER EIGHTEEN

A SWIFT RESPONSE

My friends and I were just doing quite the interesting experiment with dry ice in science class. Really, it was fascinating. But I had to cut it short when I heard all about your incredible moon rock.

May I say, it is an honor. You must have an amazing background to be connected to someone as great as Neil Armstrong! And great people are something I have a little bit of experience with.

My name's Toby Milch. I happen to be Dallas Foster's personal assistant. And he sends his most heartfelt welcome.

He also sends his regrets.

As you can imagine, there's very little Mr. Foster doesn't know about. That includes your desire to have him improve Tiger Sylvester's grades. Unfortunately, while he has great respect for your historic specimen, he's just far too busy to lend a hand.

See, Mr. Foster is currently developing an exciting new app that will revolutionize the way kids everywhere go to school. It's a tracker that uses GPS coordinates to locate bullies and other Tough Kids so our users can avoid them at all times. It's called FourEyes.

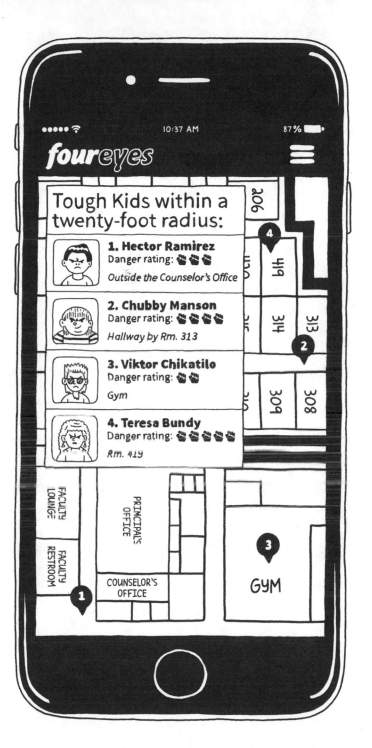

Sadly, we're running far behind our launch date, as the latest round of beta testing has revealed a number of bugs. And rewriting the code to incorporate both Objective-C and Swift to meet the new compliance standards has caused a host of issues with our dynamic allocation technique. But look at who I'm talking to! I don't need to tell a science and aeronautics buff like yourself about dynamic allocation techniques!

Of course, even if we do overcome those things in time, we still lack one major element: hard data. While the app currently tells users where Tough Kids are, it doesn't tell them where they're going to be. And in order for it to be truly effective, Mr. Foster believes it needs to be predictive. That means we need to know everything we can about the Tough Kids' habits.

Naturally, getting into their inner circle isn't easy for us, so we're at an impasse.

There's just no way we'll be able to hit our deadline.

From what I hear, you're quite resourceful. Maybe there's a way we can make this mutually beneficial?

If you were somehow able to get us the data we need on the Tough Kids, it would take days off our development time. In return, Dallas's schedule would be free enough to help Tiger. It's a win-win! And I'm sure he'd be so thrilled, he might even give you a spot on our app development team!

So, what do you think? How would you like to change the world?

CHAPTER NINETEEN

Safe Space

I am so sorry for bailing on you back there! But it's like I said in my flyer: I don't do ghosts!

Though I'm happy to hear it was just Toby Milch. And also that Dallas Foster is willing to help us if we can get data on the Tough Kids! However, that's where my joy stops.

I don't want to be the bearer of bad news, but even considering this is loco. It's hard enough to get close to a *single* Tough Kid! Do you know how hard it's going to be to worm your way inside a whole *group* of them to study their habits? You'd need to gather up all the Tough Kids in school in the safest place imaginable! And I don't even have a clue where that could possibly be!

I'm shamefaced to say it, but this is beyond my level of expertise. You are in some real, insurmountable trouble.

Hold on! That's it!

I know how we can infiltrate the Tough Kids!

OK, meet me in my office tomorrow morning before school.

I've got a special plan we're gonna put into motion.

WEDNESDAY

CHAPTER TWENTY

Law & Disorder

Morning! I'm so glad to see you made it through the night all right! And I know Lewis is overjoyed as well!

Sorry, I've got him alerting all the major outlets about a crazy new development. He's a bit overwhelmed.

So, I bet you're wondering what this is all about, huh? Well, it just so happens I've crafted an ingenious plan to help you out. And boy, is it epic.

Want to see what I did? Come on, let's go outside. You're gonna love it!

Pretty impressive, right? And if you look at the back, I signed your name to the whole thing! You are gonna be in so much trouble once this spreads around!

Hey, now, don't be mad at me! I had a really good reason for setting you up. Honest! Besides, it's not like you're gonna get suspended over this. I mean, I don't *think* you will.

Actually, come to think of it, this is pretty terrible. I might have gone a little over the top.

All right, don't freak. It might look bad, but Principal Sitz can't actually *prove* anything. When he questions you, and, well, he probably will, just follow this advice and you'll be OK!

HOW TO SURVIVE AN INTERROGATION IN THE PRINCIPAL'S OFFICE LIKE A MASTER CRIMINAL

Never admit guilt. No matter how bad the evidence looks.

. . . and we can connect your signature to samples of your handwriting from your last test! It all adds up!

Don't believe the lies.

Your buddy Max already told me everything, anyway. Yeah, he rolled on you the first chance he got. Said it was all your idea . . .

Cast guilt away from yourself by offering another suspect who might have done it.

So, there was a one-armed kid who you saw around the statue earlier this morning? Interesting.

Bargain for immunity by dangling information about a worse offense.

You're telling me you know about a major act of graffiti about to take place in this school? Well, I'd have to run it up the chain for approval, of course . . .

If the going gets really tough, turn on the secret weapon: the waterworks.

Oh no, please don't cry. Please. Oh God. Oh . . .

And, if all else fails, suggest having your parents join you. And tell the principal they're *lawyers*.

Whoa, whoa, whoa! We don't need to get any lawyers involved. Let's just keep this between us for now!

THE KEYS TO TELLING A CONVINCING LIE

Need to tell a good lie or two? I can help with that!

He's telling the truth.

BAD LIES

- "My best friend, Harry, can vouch for me. Unfortunately, it's Harry Styles, and he's on tour right now with his band. We hang out every day when he's not, though."

- "I *had* to miss class yesterday 'cuz of my astronaut training. Haven't you heard I'm gonna be the first kid going to Mars?"

- "Cheating? I wasn't cheating! I was looking at his test 'cuz I was momentarily possessed by a ghost that's been haunting my family for generations!"

KEEP IT SMALL: The bigger the lie, the more unbelievable it is.

CONVINCE YOURSELF FIRST: It's not a lie if *you* believe it.

KNOW YOUR "TELLS": Some people sweat when they lie. Some tap their feet. Whatever your "tell" is, keep it in check.

MAKE EYE CONTACT: Liars tend to avoid eye contact, so look at people directly when telling a real whopper.

GOD IS IN THE DETAILS: Paint a vivid picture for extra believability. No detail is too small.

NEVER FORGET: Commit every single one of your lies to memory. If your stories don't match up, you're as good as dead.

GOOD LIES

- "I don't recall ever doing that [*insert highly illegal thing here*]."

- "This can of spray paint? It's not mine. I'm just holding it for a friend. His name's Duane. You don't know him. He goes to another school."

- "No, I was home all night, Officer. I have no idea *who* could have set off all those fireworks outside the principal's window at two a.m."

All right, here comes Principal Sitz, right on time—just like I knew he would! And boy, is he ticked off.

Remember what I said: stay loose, proclaim your innocence, and admit to *nothing*. Do that, and you'll get through his office like it ain't no thang.

CHAPTER TWENTY-ONE
SENTENCED

I may not have enough evidence to kick your butt out of here, but I've got more than enough to hold you for an hour after school. And where you're going, they eat sixth graders like you for breakfast.

That's right. You, my friend, are about to serve a little thing we like to call . . .

Detention.

CHAPTER TWENTY-TWO

Doin' Time

Look, I'm sorry, all right? I should have told you about my plan ahead of time. I just didn't want you to back out.

See, in order to get the 411 on the Tough Kids, you need to be around a lot of 'em. And where can you find the most gathered together in one place at the same time?

Detention!

See, I told you I had you covered! Now, I know it looks terrifying, but you're perfectly safe in here. I mean, as long as the teacher's around, there's not a single thing these guys can do to harm you!

Uh-oh. OK, maybe I should have thought this out a little better!

Oh God, this plan is seriously screwed! You've got to do something quick or this could turn real ugly!

Hold on, I've got an idea. Tough Kids are usually impressed by rule breakers and outlaws, right? And you've already proven yourself by vandalizing the school statue. So, if we can just work on your attitude, I think we can pass you off as one of them!

Follow my lead and I'll show you . . .

HOW TO COME OFF LIKE A TOTAL REBEL WHEN, ON THE INSIDE, YOU JUST WANT TO CURL UP INTO A BALL AND CRY UNTIL THERE ARE NO MORE TEARS AND YOUR MOM HANDS YOU A GLASS OF WARM MILK AND YOU TAKE A NICE NAP AND THEN WATCH CARTOONS AND HUG YOUR STUFFED ANIMALS FOREVER AND EVER

Acting tough can be just that—tough. But these simple tips can take you from a quivering mound of Jell-O to a legit thug that no middle schooler would dare mess with.

LOOK THE PART

First thing you gotta do is change up your appearance. Hide anything you own that has ponies or rainbows or bright colorful patterns on it. Think dark. *Real dark.* Mess up your hair. Give yourself a couple of bruises and fake tattoos and scars. (See the sidebar on page 134.) Tear your clothes a bit. In fact, tear off your sleeves completely. Sleeves are for wimps. If you do it right, you should look like you just spent a night in county lockup.

BEFORE

Hi, there!

AFTER

What're **you** lookin' at?

GET SOME BADITUDE

Tough Kids don't smile or laugh. Not unless it's at someone else's misfortune. And they don't care about anything, let alone what the world thinks of 'em. Life? Death? It's all the same. So put away your sunny disposition and desire to impress, and replace it with a gritty, gnarly attitude. Squint your eyes a little. Growl. It helps to think of everything you encounter as an inconvenience you'd be *this close* to punching away if only The Man wouldn't stop you.

DON'T SAY A LOT

Being the strong, silent type projects confidence and toughness. It also creates an air of mystery you can use to your advantage. Start by planting some dark rumors about yourself—the more insane, the better. And then don't acknowledge them. Soon, the mystery surrounding you will grow to epic proportions and students will even add to your myth, making you tougher than you could ever seem on your own!

HOW TO CREATE A REALISTIC SCAR IN MINUTES

Works like a dream!

WHAT YOU'LL NEED

- **Rubber cement**
- **A toothpick**
- **Red, purple, and pink markers or makeup**

STEPS

1. **Apply rubber cement to the area where you want the scar and let it dry.**
2. **Use the toothpick to scrape away a jagged line inside the rubber cement. This will be your scar.**
3. **Fill in the scar with either markers or makeup to look as realistic as possible.**
4. **Apply a second coat of rubber cement over the scar and let it dry.**
5. **Use the toothpick to lightly scratch into the scar a little bit more.**
6. **Recolor your scar ever so slightly with the markers or makeup.**
7. **Fool everyone.**

LANGUAGE

Finally, *how* you say things is just as important as *what* you say. To appear tougher, lower your voice a few octaves and make it sound gravelly, like you've spent the past two years working in a coal mine. And avoid cutesy phrases or proper grammar. That's for Nerds.

PHRASES TO AVOID

"I got a boo-boo!"

"Who wants to get tickled?"

"Mommy, help me!"

"Can we talk about our feelings for a minute?"

"I'm telling on you!"

"Hug party! Who's in?"

PHRASES TO USE

"What are we destroying today?"

"You talkin' to me?"

"Back in juvie . . ."

"Anyone else feel like breaking something?"

"Detention? I ain't got time for detention."

Unintelligible grunting

All right, I've toughened you up as best I can. Now let's go talk to these guys. Hopefully, they'll recognize you as one of their own!

CHAPTER TWENTY-THREE

KNUCKLES CRACKED

You could totally fit in with our crew. Yeah, you'd be a great lookout. You could come with us everywhere and be down with all kinds of stuff we get ourselves into. It'd be tight. And God knows we could use some new blood—especially since **Neck Bone** just got expelled and his dad's sending him away to boarding school.

Problem is, as tough as you seem, I heard that other new kid, Freddy Dugan, is still tormenting you. And having a kid who's getting bullied in our group? That'd make us look like a bunch of scrubs. It's a no-go.

Although . . .

I wonder if there's a way we could let it slide? I mean, there *might* be. That is, *if* you can make something happen for *us*.

See, I got my own issue that could use a good pounding. It's a bit delicate, so I'd appreciate it if you kept it under wraps.

Ready to hear it?

All right, check this out:

I got a sister your age. Bernice. She's havin' a real tough go of it here in middle school. She's not like us, you know? She's sensitive. Bright. She's . . . she's . . .

The girl's a saint.

Sob.
Sob.

Sorry for getting all emotional. It's just . . . when I think of what that little angel's been through . . .

Anyway, it's her birthday on Saturday. And she's having a party. Only, no one's RSVP'd. If she opens that door and the place is empty? Well, I just couldn't bear the look on her face.

But I know the whole school would attend if the two most popular kids—Darnell and Caitlin—did. And that's where you come in. If you can find some way to get them to go, I'd be forever in your debt. You could roll with us anytime, no questions asked.

And here, you can give them *these* to help.

A kid traded them to me this morning in exchange for some "protection." I heard Darnell and Caitlin are really into this group. I'd offer 'em up myself, but if Bernice ever found out, she'd murder me. That's why someone like you who's outside my usual gang would be perfect. With your convincing and these tickets, that just might be enough.

So, how about it? Make Bernice's birthday one she'll remember, and we'll be thick as thieves. Make my kid sister cry, and her birthday will be one *you'll* remember. Forever.

CHAPTER TWENTY-FOUR

Tickets to Despair

Let me just say right now, for the record, that I am in awe of you. For real, that was dope what you just did back there! Seriously. Those Tough Kids are . . . well . . . *tough.* Not anyone coulda faked it like that with them. And these tickets in your hands are your salvation! Whatever you do, keep them guarded at all costs, because if you lose them then you'll be totally, 100 percent, without a doubt scr—

Argh! Freddy and Kevin again! And Freddy didn't even have detention! He must have stayed late just to mess with you!

You can't hide from me. Wherever you go, I will chew you up.

Hmm . . . I think you could sell that a bit more. It's like, I **heard** you, but I didn't entirely **believe** you.

Well, what if I ate these too? You know, to drive home the point?

Yeah, but if they're destroyed then you lose any bargaining power they hold.

See, that's why you're the best!

Ooh, these guys don't know when to quit!

These tickets seem important to you. Too bad you'll **never** get them back. HA-HA-HA-HA-HA!

Much better! Now **that**, I believed!

This is a major problem.

Look, I've tried my best not to stoop to Kevin Carl's level, but we've got to get those tickets back. Otherwise, the only food you'll ever eat again will be out of a straw! And if I have to completely ruin another kid's life to do so, then God help me, I will. 'Cuz now this isn't just about survival. This is about revenge.

Meet me in my office tomorrow morning. I promise you this: Freddy Dugan and Kevin Carl are going down.

THURSDAY

CHAPTER TWENTY-FIVE
Breaking In

I hope you're feeling well rested! Not everyone in this office

is. Right, Lewis?

Sorry, he gets a bit irritable when he's tired. And, believe me, that's totally understandable—I had him working all through the night to dig up dirt on Kevin Carl. And he got *everything*. His parents' names. His cats' names. His first-grade teachers' names. If it was online, he found it! And why, you might ask? Oh, just for this:

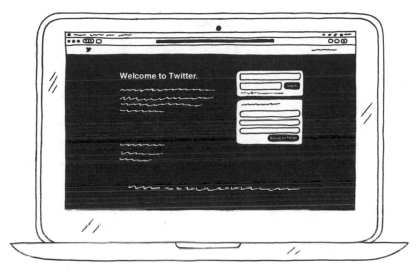

We're gonna hack Kevin's Twitter account!

Pretty awesome, right?

See, I know that Kevin sends Direct Messages to Freddy throughout the day on Twitter, giving him advice and guidance. And I was thinking, what if Kevin gave Freddy some bad advice? But not just *any* bad advice. I'm talking about some seriously, colossally nuclear-meltdown-terrible advice! Something that would backfire so abysmally, their little bromance would explode faster than a stick of dynamite in the sun! Ooh, I'm drooling just thinking about it! And all we have to do is find a way into Kevin's Twitter account.

Now, normally this would be a difficult operation, but I happen to have some experience in this arena. Let's just say I didn't get an A in U.S. history solely by sleeping through it all semester. And I'm gonna show you everything I know.

So, grab your phone and warm up your thumbs. Here's . . .

HOW TO HACK YOUR ENEMY'S PASSWORDS

Guessing an unknown password can be easier than you think. Here are the password suggestions you can try:

COMMON PASSWORDS

People aren't as unique as they seem; a lot of 'em use the same passwords. Start guessing by using this list of SplashData's top twenty-five most common ones.*

1. 123456
2. password
3. 12345678
4. qwerty
5. abc123
6. 123456789
7. 111111
8. 1234567
9. iloveyou
10. adobe123
11. 123123
12. admin
13. 1234567890
14. letmein
15. photoshop
16. 1234
17. monkey
18. shadow
19. sunshine
20. 12345
21. password1
22. princess
23. azerty
24. trustno1
25. 000000

*This list comes from http://splashdata.com/press/worstpasswords2013.htm.

NAMES

If those don't work, names are another common password to use. Try your target's first name or his or her best friend's, girlfriend's, or boyfriend's. Or, if they're older, try their wife's, husband's, or kids' names! In fact, even their pets' names might work! If you don't know this information,

Google it or check out your target's Facebook account. Chances are, they've probably mentioned it!

DATES

Important dates like birthdays or anniversaries are also common passwords. Again, most of this stuff is easy to find on the Internet with a simple search if you don't already know it.

CAPITALIZATION

Passwords often need at least one capital letter. If the passwords on page 147 don't work, try them again by capitalizing only the first letter.

ZEROS AND ONES

Finally, a lot of sites require a number in the password. But guess what? People aren't good with numbers, so most of them just put a 0 or a 1 at the beginning or end of theirs. So, if you haven't guessed their password yet, run through all the previous options and add a 0 or 1 before or after. There's a good chance that may just be it!

I haven't cracked it yet. Have you?

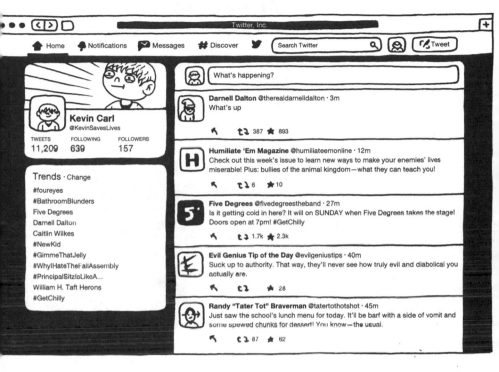

You never cease to amaze me! And now that we have access to Kevin's Direct Messages, something tells me he has some *pretty interesting* advice he'd like to give Freddy. And by "interesting," I mean "horrible." And by "horrible," I mean "catastrophic."

Care to do the honors?

CHAPTER TWENTY-SIX

YIELD SIGNS

Do you know what that idiot told me to do? He said that in order to be more popular, I should ask out Brittany Osborn, the cutest girl in school! And the best way to do that would be to go to her first-period class and *serenade her with a Five Degrees song* in front of *everybody*! And not just that—he said that I should also make sure she knew I was serious by doing a dance routine to go with it and then presenting her with a drawing of the two of us kissing with the words "I love you more than my mommy" written underneath it. Well, that did not go well. Not at all. Brittany laughed so hard at me that snot came out of her nose. And the rest of the class was laughing too. Even Mrs. Hansen! And they all made kissy noises! The only way to escape them was to run out and hide out in the janitor's closet! And then I didn't realize it had locked from the outside, so I was trapped in it for thirty minutes until someone found me! I thought I was gonna die!

Here! You can have your stupid tickets back!

Clearly, I shouldn't have followed Kevin's advice. And I'm gonna make sure everyone else in this school knows just how bad it is too! As far as I'm concerned, his business is over!

CHAPTER TWENTY-SEVEN

2 Cool 4 School

Oh, that was a thing of beauty! I've never seen a kid that upset before! Even when Nick Totino got pantsed during his student council campaign speech and everyone saw his Donald Duck underwear!

What? Don't tell me you actually feel sorry for that orangutan. He earned his fate the minute he decided to worship Kevin Carl—it's not my fault he chose the dark side. And look, here comes Kevin now!

Man, that felt good. I think I might even skip dessert this evening, 'cuz the revenge I'm tasting is already so, so sweet. Aw, who am I kidding, I can't resist chocolate pudding!

But hold on, it's not time to crack open a cup just yet. We've still got to make Knuckles's sister's birthday party a hit by getting Darnell and Caitlin to attend. Once that's accomplished and the Tough Kids are on your side, all the other cliques will fall in line too and you'll be home free!

However, as you probably guessed, getting Darnell and Caitlin to stop by is gonna be tougher than the Tough Kids' reputation. Not only are they going to be next to impossible to convince, but it's going to be just as difficult to even talk to them, period. See, no one gets within ten feet of Darnell and Caitlin unless you're already middle school royalty. And, sorry to say, but you're still a peasant around here.

However, as usual, I may have a way around it.

I heard from a good source that Darnell and Caitlin are ditching third period today to hang out in the woods behind the school. They'll be alone for forty minutes. And they might actually listen to you instead of pretending like you don't exist. It's the perfect time to approach them!

Of course, in order to talk to them, that means you'll have to skip class too.

Look, I know it's risky, but you're so close! You just need to get through this, and you'll be set for the rest of your middle school life! And there's no other time but now! Trust me on this! I haven't let you down yet, have I?

Shoot! There's the bell! Look, we only have a couple minutes. I need to know now, are you in or are you out?

Awesomesauce!

OK, now follow my lead, 'cuz you and I are bustin' outta

here!

HOW TO DITCH CLASS LIKE A NINJA

Ditching class is no walk in the park. Which is funny, 'cuz I often ditch class to take a walk in the park. To get started, you'll need several things:

AN ALIBI

An unexcused absence can result in a school-wide manhunt, so an alibi is a lifesaver. If you've got one of those teachers who never pays attention, have a friend answer for you or fake your signature during roll call. If you're good with impressions, try calling the school secretary, pretending to be your parent excusing yourself from class.

SAFE HOUSES

On the off chance you're spotted while ditching, it's vital to have a good hiding place to duck into until the heat cools off. Consider:

- **THE BATHROOM.** Discreet, and teachers of the opposite sex won't be able to come in. Might not want to hang out in there too long, though, unless your sense of smell isn't very good.

- **THE JANITOR'S CLOSET.** Creepy and usually locked, but very secure if you need a little more time and can gain access.

- **THE LIBRARY.** The tall stacks can provide great cover for a middle schooler in need.

A HALL PASS

Save your old hall passes just in case you run into any teachers. Or fake one with some colored paper that matches the school's and make random scribbles on it. Most employees are so overworked and exhausted, they won't even notice it's a fake if you flash it quickly enough!

EXCUSES

In case anyone does stop and question you, it's important to have a good excuse prepared for why you're out of class. A great trick is to say that you're headed to the principal's office. Who's going to think a kid would lie about that? Whatever you decide, make sure you commit it to memory. The last thing you want is to be caught off guard and panic.

Once you're ready to ditch, do it in the following manner:

KEEP COOL

You know who looks guilty? Guilty people. Instead of sneaking around like a criminal, walk confidently like a person with nothing to hide.

DON'T RUN

Never run. Ever. You might as well put a sign around your neck reading "Bust me." Remember, if you've done your planning

correctly, you'll already have a good excuse and a fake hall pass to help you if a teacher stops you. Use them. That's what they're there for.

TAKE THE ROAD LESS TRAVELED

Lastly, scope out your possible routes. Keep logs of teachers' comings and goings and record the amount of traffic certain hallways have. Then plan and execute your escape using the directions with the smallest chance of running into anyone. Sometimes the shortest distance is not the safest!

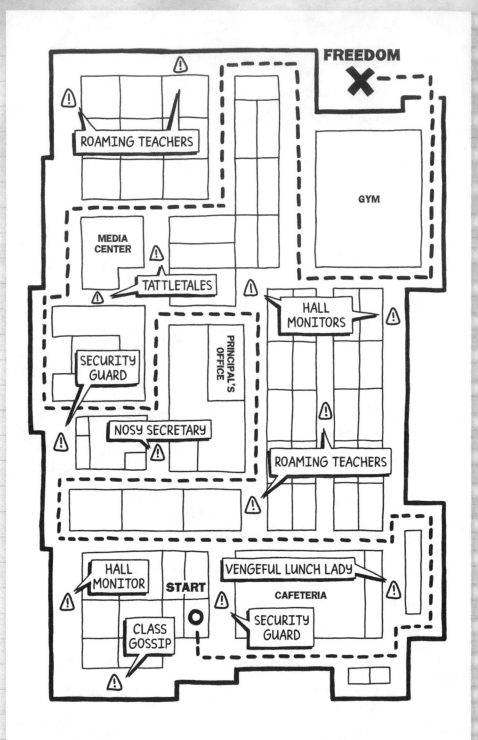

ALMS TO G EASE

Skipping class takes more than big *cojones*; it can also take some unwitting accomplices. Cozying up to these people can ensure your safe travels!

SECURITY OFFICERS
Get on their good sides and they'll be less likely to see your bad one when ditching class.

All clear!

THE SCHOOL NURSE
Nobody understands your "nervous stomach" like her. If you do get caught, you can lie and say you were on the way to pay her a visit.

Just stay in my office till you feel better, hon.

THE CLASS TATTLETALE
Sure, he might be annoying, but if having him in your corner keeps him from blabbing his big mouth, you're way ahead of the game.

I refuse to believe you'd do **anything** wrong.

THE JANITOR
He knows all the dirty secrets of the school. Literally. He's cleaned them. And he might not rat yours out if you're good to him.

Looks like you got yourself in another mess. Good thing I'm here to help you clean up.

THE CLASS ARTIST
He might be moody and demanding, but he sure can forge a good hall pass!

My greatest work yet!

HALL PASS

We made it! Can you taste that sweet air of freedom? I don't think I can ever go back! I can't! I won't! I—

No. No. Gotta remember what we're here for. Darnell and Caitlin. And there they are, right where I knew they'd be.

Now go over and talk to them. I just hope Knuckles's tickets are enough for them to agree to come to the party.

CHAPTER TWENTY-EIGHT
The Price of Popularity

I'm sorry, but did you honestly think we would ever attend such a lame event as Bernice's birthday party? Have you even *seen* her? She's got a full-on mustache, and I'm pretty sure she eats paint chips. For real. Her mouth's always blue.

Look, it's not gonna happen, OK? You can't buy popularity. You have to earn it by being the best. That means going to only the coolest parties and the most exclusive events and the trendiest affairs and—

Sorry, it's just . . . stupid Ashley Greenblatt's bat mitzvah! It's happening this weekend too and anyone who's anyone is going. Except for us. That's 'cuz Mr. Singh is gonna call our parents and tell them how bad we've been in his class, and when they find out, we're toast. They told us if one more teacher calls them, we are totally grounded. And if we can't attend, that little show-off Jessica Myers and her stupid boyfriend, Kyle, are gonna be the most popular kids in school! And we hate them!

What makes it more unfair is that our parents will automatically believe whatever Mr. Singh says, just 'cuz he's a teacher. They think he walks on water! They won't even listen to our side of the story! And boy, do we have one.

See, Mr. Singh isn't as perfect as parents think he is. He plays favorites, tests you on things that aren't in the book, and even chews gum in class when we're not allowed to. He's a total hypocrite. We even wrote a funny article with the help of the Class Clowns about him, 'cuz we're not that great with jokes but they rock at 'em. Plus, they totally wanna hang with us, so it's no biggie.

Anyway, the plan was to put it in the school paper anonymously. If the paper published it, our parents would finally believe us that Mr. Singh's not a saint and that he's exaggerating all of our problems. But then we realized the editor would never let us.

If only there was some way to sneak it in there.

Tell you what, an idea just popped into our heads. Maybe we can strike a bargain and stop by Bernice's on the way to the bat mitzvah. We can't stay long, but it could get you what you need. But we'll only go if you can find a way to get our article into the school paper. It's gotta print tomorrow, though, before the Fall Assembly, and we can't be linked to it in any way.

So, how about it? If you can do this for us, we'll put in an appearance at this lame party. Cross us, though, and we'll make sure you're the least popular kid in school. And, considering some of the scrubs here, that's saying a lot.

So?

CHAPTER TWENTY-NINE

Dirty Business

Holy crap, I don't know how you talked them into it, but you did it! This is it! Everything we've been working toward! All the cliques are lined up exactly where you want them to be. You just need to help Darnell and Caitlin get their article into the school paper, and the dominoes will all fall into place.

Problem is, you are totally, 100 percent, without-a-doubt boned.

See, what they're asking for is a lot harder than you think. Actually, it's impossible—even for me. I don't know if you know, but Mrs. Appleton runs the school paper. And she's so observant, we'd never be able to sneak into her class. Plus, even if we could miraculously get in, we'll never get the article past her. She looks over *everything* and would rather die than let anything criticizing a teacher go to print. Even if it was *true!*

I'm sorry, but we've got to find another way to buy

Darnell and Caitlin off. Maybe we could try getting them a guest spot on their favorite TV show! I mean, I'm sure they'd love that, and TV shows must let regular, untrained child actors have walk-on parts on their shows at the very last minute, right?

Aw, who am I kidding? We might as well dig our own graves and lie down inside of 'em.

Wait a second! That could work!

To get their article into the paper, we need someone on the *inside*. Someone on the staff who Mrs. Appleton trusts enough to give them access to the paper after she's approved it, but who's shady enough to agree to sneak Darnell and Caitlin's article in.

One major problem, though: there's only one kid in this school who possesses that kind of duplicity, scheming, and access. I'm warning you, you're not going to like who it is. Are you absolutely sure you want to go ahead with this plan?

OK, then let's go see him. His locker's right around the corner. But don't say I didn't warn you.

See? I said you weren't gonna like it.

CHAPTER THIRTY

A Clean Slate

I gotta hand it to ya, you really got my number with that whole Freddy situation. Because of that debacle, my entire client base is abandoning me left and right. But I guess you knew that would happen.

Look, I know we started off on the wrong foot, but this has gone too far. I owe you an apology. And Max too. The truth is, I never wanted to compete with him.

And I certainly didn't want to ruin your life either. I just wanted to be seen as an equal for once. I mean, Max is so good at what he does! It's intimidating!

That's why I left in the first place. It wasn't to be his rival. It was to prove I could do it myself. But I can't. No one can. Max showed me everything I know, and I lost sight of that. But now my vision's restored.

Maybe I could come back and Max and I could be partners again? If he'll let me. We could shake middle school up like we always intended to! Give it the one-two punch it really needs! And we could start with you. Your success will be our crowning achievement. It'll be legendary!

Just tell me what you want. *Anything.* And I'll make it happen.

CHAPTER THIRTY—ONE

Working Things Out

Sniff.
Sniff.

What? No, those aren't tears! I just pulled a muscle, OK? Like, a really bad one! Like, a groin or something! I was doing a lot of calisthenics before school!

Anyway, I'm really happy Kevin and I were able to patch things up. And I owe it all to you. You're the best client I've ever had. No, you're more than just a client—you're my friend. And now you're going to be a middle school boss!

Kevin says he needs until tomorrow morning to work his magic and sneak the article into the paper. So just sit tight and enjoy your evening off. We'll meet up in the morning to move this plan into the endgame.

FRIDAY

CHAPTER THIRTY-TWO

A Good Day to Be Alive

And why am I so pumped? Only 'cuz Kevin Carl made good on his word. I don't know how, but he got the article published. Your survival is guaranteed!

That makes two of us!

All that's left now is for you to go to class. I'll see you after first period, when the paper comes out, to celebrate. And when it's published, I'm sure everyone will be wondering who the anonymous people were behind the amazing article that rocked the school!

CHAPTER THIRTY-THREE

Betrayed

What? No! Why were Darnell and Caitlin's names published? We told Kevin a million times it had to run anonymously. I just don't understand.

Unless . . .

Oh no. Oh no, no, no, no, no, no, no, no, no. It can't be! Don't you get it?

Kevin must have set you up! He put Darnell and Caitlin's names back in! He wanted our plan to fail!

What is he talking about? You didn't do a comic!

Oh my God! He made a comic with your name on it! That's bad. That's really bad. And I can only imagine how this is all gonna look to Darnell and Caitlin!

And it won't just be them! Without Darnell and Caitlin's help, you can't keep any of the promises you made to the other cliques either! This is gonna cause a chain reaction the likes I've never seen!

I'm so sorry! Quick, we've got to get you out of here before the entire school turns on you!

Oh God. Is it getting hot in here? I can't breathe! My whole left side is numb! I . . . I don't know what to do! There's literally no way this could possibly get any worse!

And yet . . .

CHAPTER THIRTY-FOUR

BUSTED!

I knew you were a bad apple. And now you're on your third strike. The only thing left to do is confess.

I want to hear it all. Every bad thing you've done since you've been here. All the lying. The stealing. The cutting class. *Everything.* You do this and *maybe* I won't

expel you. Maybe, when your parents come
after the Fall Assembly, you'll just be
suspended instead.

Well? I'm waiting.

Nothing, huh? Figures. I assume you're
still taking Max's advice, then. Such a shame.

You're not the first kid he's done this to,
you know? Max loves to corrupt the students
and turn them against me. It brings him such

delight. I just wish my boy thought better of me than that.

Oh, what? You didn't know? You mean, all this time, you've been following his advice and breaking rules left and right and he never once mentioned to you the fact that . . .

CHAPTER THIRTY-FIVE

Unfriended

Are you OK? Jeez, you look like you just saw the secret ingredients to the school lunch meat! What happened in there?
Did he call your parents? Torture you? What?

He told you,
didn't he?

OK, OK, yes, it's true, but I have a good reason I never
mentioned he was my dad. It's just I—!

Wait, what do you mean I ruined your life?

No, I didn't! Everything I've done is to help you! You're the one who hired *me*, remember?

You know, you're the most ungrateful person I've ever met! I've been busting my hump to help you since you first got here, and all you've done is whine and cry about being a good kid the entire time! You haven't appreciated anything I've done! And I've put my neck on the line for you!

Oh, so you don't need me anymore, huh? Yeah? Well, I don't need you either!

You know, I can't believe I even thought we were friends! We're not friends and we never were. You were just my client. And you know what? As of this moment, I officially *quit*.

The Fall Assembly's in an hour. Good luck finding someone else to get you out of all this trouble now. 'Cuz guess what? You're gonna need it.

CHAPTER THIRTY-SIX

The Fall Assembly

Why am I not surprised? Well, don't get too comfy. I've already found a new client. And he shows *way more* promise than you ever did.

Aw, who am I kidding? Eugene's *hopeless*.

Look, I'm sorry about what I said back there. I just... I just got mad is all. I didn't mean any of it. You're not just a client. You *are* my friend.

The reason I never told you about my dad is because being the principal's son sucks. That's why I go by my mom's maiden name. And all this stuff I've been teaching you? It's essential.

See, life isn't easy. People are going to tell you what to do, what to think, and how to behave. If it's not your parents, it's your teachers, or your boss, or your family, or the government. And as hard as middle school is, it only gets harder. You'll grow up and have responsibilities and bills and mortgages and taxes. It's enough to beat anyone down. That's what happened to my dad. He wasn't always like this. He used to be nice.

I don't want that to happen to me, or you. And sure, there are risks with all of this. Sometimes you win, sometimes you eat pavement. But today? Today is not that day.

Listen, I can still get you out of all this. I know it! Just give me another shot. You don't have to forgive me. You don't have to be friends with me again. All you have to do is trust me. I've only ever wanted to help you. Will you give me one last chance?

Excellent! I won't let you down! I promise!

Now, I've got an amazing plan to get you out of this mess. Ready to hear it?

You and I . . .

. . . are gonna wreck the Fall Assembly.

CHAPTER THIRTY-SEVEN

Easily Distracted

It's perfect! See, *everyone* hates the Fall Assembly. And ruining it would stick it to my dad hard-core. You'd be legendary! And if this works out the way I'm planning, you'll also get out of trouble!

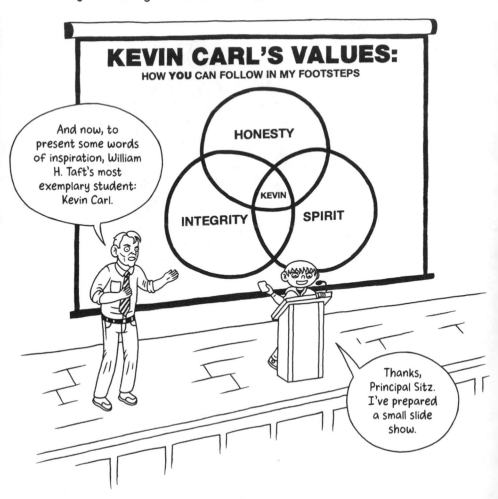

And it all hinges on him. Kevin Carl. We're gonna finally take him down, once and for all. And here's how:

See ol' Eugene over here? Well, I didn't just recruit him for his charm. I also wanted his cell phone. I knew you and I would make up eventually, so after you left, I pretended to message Kevin as Eugene. See, "Eugene" was thinking about maybe hiring me instead of Kevin, and let's just say Kevin made quite the compelling argument against it. I've got everything I need to wipe him out. I just have to connect my new slide show to the AV booth without anyone noticing.

And that's where you come in.

In order to swap Kevin's slides for my own, I need you to create a distraction for me. And it's gotta be big! Something that'll wreak havoc! Of course, you know I've got a few suggestions:

HOW TO CREATE THE ULTIMATE DISTRACTION

Misdirection is an essential part of every middle schooler's "tool belt." While people aren't paying attention, you or your *partner can swipe something important, plant evidence, or just bolt if you're in trouble. These are my favorite methods:*

PULL THE FIRE ALARM

It's the oldest trick in the book. One good pull and the entire school will be forced to stop, drop, and roll out of the building. You can get away with anything you want in the ensuing panic.

UNLEASH A WILD ANIMAL

Science teachers keep weird pets like snakes or rats in their classrooms on occasion. Get hold of one (or bring your own from home), let it loose in the crowd, and do your thang as chaos ensues!

THE PUKE-A-THON

You ever see someone puke and it's so gross it makes you blow chunks too? Well, imagine doing that during a school assembly! I'm talkin' Hurl City! Now, *that's* a distraction! To puke on command, just do what always works for me: think about your least favorite teacher naked! If that doesn't do the trick, you can try my fake-puke recipe—it's the bomb! (See the sidebar on the facing page.)

RUFUS THE JANITOR'S FAKE-VOMIT RECIPE

Need to conjure up some fake vomit? Try Rufus the Janitor's famous recipe!

Use it wisely, child!

Planning time:
2 days

Actual prep time:
15 minutes

Ingredients:
1 cup chocolate milk
1 cup leftovers from last night's dinner
¾ cup cooked oatmeal
5 crackers (optional)
Long-sleeved shirt

Directions:
2 days before:

1. Fill a large glass with chocolate milk. Leave out, unrefrigerated.

The night before:

2. Secretly collect leftovers from dinner. Hide them.

The morning of:

3. Collect chocolate milk from step 1. It should be sour and a little lumpy. Collect leftovers, oatmeal, and crackers, if using.

4. Mix ingredients in a small bowl with a spoon. Pour into a large paper cup and seal tightly with plastic wrap and rubber bands. Wear a long-sleeved shirt that day. Hide in your shirtsleeve. Go to school.

5. When ready, secretly remove plastic wrap. Start retching and hold your sleeve to your face. Bend over and pour fake vomit out as you make convincing noises.

6. Kick back and enjoy the results as chaos ensues!

MAKE A SCENE

Finally, you can create some drama by just making a good ol'-fashioned scene. Anything can work, so long as it's shocking and disruptive enough to get a lot of attention.

MAX'S TOP 5 SCENES

Pretend you're being attacked by invisible bees.

Run around in your underwear while singing "She'll Be Comin' Round the Mountain."

**Break up with someone LOUDLY.
(Bonus points if you're not even dating.)**

Cry quietly for no discernible reason and then tell everyone to ignore you, but keep crying anyway.

Suddenly bust out a sweet break-dancing routine to end all break-dancing routines.

Now go out there and really create some chaos. The bigger, the better! Let's just pray it distracts everyone long enough so I can make the swap.

CHAPTER THIRTY-EIGHT
DOWNWARD SLIDE

As for you, new kid, your days of disruption
and troublemaking are over. If you thought
I was hard on you before, when your par-

ents get here you'll wish you had never set foot in middle school. It's too bad, because you could have been a decent human being like Kevin Carl. He's everything a student should be. Honest, sincere, loyal, and—

What's going on here?

CHAPTER THIRTY-NINE

Dialing It Up

Thanks to your distraction, Kevin's new slide show is up and running. And boy, is it revealing. There are things he'd never want the school to know. Things like:

Or . . .

And then there's this . . .

But we're not done yet. There's one final slide. The pièce de résistance!

OK, actually that last one's just a Photoshop job I had Lewis do a while back. Not bad, right? And I think the school agrees.

This is far better than I could have ever imagined!

In all my years, I have never . . . I . . . You might not have drawn that comic, but you still ruined my assembly! And I can get you on that alone! In five minutes, you'll be going down farther than—

Not so fast, Dad.

If you suspend the new kid, you'll have to suspend Kevin too.

And if you were wrong about your precious star pupil, think about how many other kids you misjudged.

Good kids. Middle schoolers who just wanted to make their horrible lives a little better.

He does make an interesting point.

I'll tell you what. I'll lift my suspension. For now.

I'm warning you, though: if you thought I was bad before, just you wait. This is End Times. From now on, I'll be following you closer than a bloodhound on the scent of a badger doused in cologne in an empty wood without trees. One false move and it's over.

Now get out of my face before I regret my decision. And I'm already starting to.

CHAPTER FORTY-ONE

Survival Guaranteed

Whew! That was a close one. But I knew I'd get you out of trouble. Only, you can't celebrate yet. There's still the matter of Darnell and Caitlin to deal with.

Funny they should ask. Because, if I recall, there was a really dope party we were planning on attending on Saturday. A girl by the name of Bernice. And we kinda needed them to stop by. Maybe you should ask if they'll reconsider?

And there you have it. The popular kids agree to go to the party, pleasing the Tough Kids; who let you gather data for the Nerds; who tutor Tiger Sylvester for the Jocks; who, in turn, throw the football game for the Preps; who finance our crusade to buy chocolate for the Band Geeks; who, as a result, let Eraser Head make his masterpiece; who then convinces his Artist friends to draw the Class Clowns' comic strips; and you, my good friend, are the person who made it all happen.

Told ya I had you covered. *Now* it's time to get down.

SATURDAY

CHAPTER FORTY-TWO

Partay!

Thanks to my expert advice, you're now the most popular kid in school. This might as well be *your* party—I don't think there's a single kid who doesn't like you.

You know, you're not a total scrub. That's the highest praise I can give someone.

We should hang sometime. I'll "draw up" some plans. Heh-heh.

Spring break in Tahiti. In or out?

When Mr. Foster's app goes public, you're totally getting stock options.

And this shindig's pretty happening. I mean, you managed to get *everyone* here. Even Lewis made it! Although it's too bad that birthday cake contained so much dairy. I don't think it's agreeing with him.

Looks like it's working out for all of us. Except, of course, for Kevin Carl. He's now the *least* popular kid in school. Even Eugene Leach is higher up on the social totem pole, thanks to his role in Kevin's downfall. And who'd have thought *that* would happen?

Why, it's almost as if this whole thing was planned from the very start. Yes, indeed. Like some genius mastermind concocted it.

Hey, now! Easy there... Easy...

Look, I knew you would have never agreed to it if you had *all* the details from the beginning. Seriously, you can't just rule the school by making a few friends. You gotta do something epic. Legendary. And I promised you, you wouldn't just survive. I promised you'd be a boss. And I'm a man of my word.

Gotta say, though, you went above and beyond. I think you've got a real knack for this kind of rule-breaking stuff. You could go far.

Let me ask you a question: have you ever thought about politics? 'Cuz I think you could be class president. And I happen to know a pretty good campaign manager. Or haven't you opened up your invitation?

And I've got an amazing strategy to get you elected. I'm warning you, though, there will be a certain amount of risk involved. But you know that old saying: without risk, there's no reward. Besides, something tells me, with my help, you'll have no problem getting elected.

TO BE

CONTINUED . . .

Acknowledgments

If surviving middle school is hard, crafting a book is almost as difficult. Luckily, I had some great people to help me along the way. First and foremost I'd like to thank Laura Geringer Bass for her keen insights, guidance, and support throughout the entirety of this book. I'd also like to thank Justin Rucker and Tamara Shannon for helping me navigate the waters of publishing and lending their expertise when I needed it most.

Charles Kochman deserves a huge shout-out for believing in me and my material enough to make this thing a reality and for shepherding it along the way. I'm lucky enough to have found a great editor in Erica Finkel, who got exactly what I was trying to do and gave me plenty of room to write the book the way I envisioned it, yet also asked all the right questions and poked holes in all the things that needed poking. Chad W. Beckerman, of course, also deserves huge thanks for championing my book well before it was a book and, once it was, for lending his great designer's eye and vision to making it feel unique and awesome. I'd also like to thank Jen Graham for keeping things on schedule, Richard Slovak for catching all my many grammatical mistakes, Kathy Lovisolo for ensuring the book printed well and looked its best, Morgan Dubin for her marketing and publicity expertise, and Gabriella DeGennaro for her helpful notes.

In my research department, I'd like to thank Anna Goodell, who let me ask her all kinds of embarrassing questions so I could get into the mind of a sixth grader.

Finally, I'd like to thank Sally Mason for her support, for listening to me pitch countless iterations of plots and schemes, and for generally putting up with me while I was working on this.

Thanks so much to all of you. Without you, this book would have turned out far differently.

About the Author

NEIL SWAAB is a Brooklyn-based illustrator whose work has appeared in the *New York Times, Utne Reader,* the *Village Voice,* and most recently James Patterson's *Middle School: My Brother Is a Big, Fat Liar.* Swaab has worked on Adult Swim's *Superjail!,* Comedy Central's *Ugly Americans,* and Cartoon Network's *Annoying Orange.* He is also a syndicated cartoonist whose comic strip appeared online and in print for thirteen years. Learn more about Swaab at neilswaab.com.